Troslava

TWO LINES
PRESS

Damir Karakaš

Translated from Croatian
by Ellen Elias-Bursać

Celebration

Originally published as *Proslava*;
this translation of *Celebration* is published by arrangement with Ampi
Margini Literary Agency and with the authorization of Damir Karakaš.
© Damir Karakaš, 2019
Translation © 2024 by Ellen Elias-Bursać

Two Lines Press
www.twolinespress.com

ISBN 978-1-949641-66-0
Ebook ISBN 978-1-949641-67-7

Cover design by Crisis
Typeset by Stephanie Nisbet

Library of Congress Cataloging-in-Publication Data
Names: Karakaš, Damir, author. | Elias-Bursać, Ellen, translator.
Title: Celebration/Damir Karakaš; translated from Croatian by Ellen
Elias-Bursać.
Other titles: *Proslava*. English
Description: San Francisco, CA: Two Lines Press, 2024.
Identifiers: LCCN 2023058008 (print) | LCCN 2023058009 (ebook)
| ISBN 9781949641660 (paperback) | ISBN 9781949641677 (ebook)
Subjects: LCGFT: Novels.
Classification: LCC PG1619.21.A638 P7613 2024 (print) | LCC
PG1619.21.A638 (ebook) | DDC 891.8/336--dc23/eng/20240507
LC record available at https://lccn.loc.gov/2023058008
LC ebook record available at https://lccn.loc.gov/2023058009

1 3 5 7 9 10 8 6 4 2

This book was published with the financial support of the Ministry of
Culture and Media of the Republic of Croatia, and is supported in part
by an award from the National Endowment for the Arts.

Republika
Hrvatska
Ministarstvo
kulture
i medija
*Republic
of Croatia
Ministry
of Culture
and Media*

House

Night, a black forest, a skeletal arm suddenly loomed up before him; he grabbed his rifle and yelled: "You'll never catch me!" When he pulled the trigger, he woke and propped himself slowly up on his elbows: with one eye he watched, with the other he listened; then he sank slowly back down into the soft dip between the two gold-leafed beech trees.

Wrapped in a gray army blanket, he lay there, trying again to propel his gaze through the fog, but still he couldn't see a thing; after the first patch, a denser fog had rolled in and he couldn't even see his own rifle next to his long, numb limbs. In silence he began again to listen; he cupped his hand to his ear to better catch the sounds: deep in his ears throbbed the sinews of the trees. After a little bit a breeze picked up, it grew stronger, colder; at one moment the wind deep in the forest seemed to be thrumming through someone's hollow bones; the thought flashed through his mind of all the human bones that would be carried off by beasts for years after the war.

The sun woke him; it scorched so harshly that he had to take his canteen, wet his hand, and rub the white-hot nape of his neck; then the sunlight flashed traitorously on the barrel of his rifle so he drew it quickly under the frayed edge of the blanket; he squirmed his way deeper in among the branches, arranged several of them in front of his nose to be as out of sight as possible, and his yellow-brown Ustaša uniform—that had some calling them tawny cats—melded perfectly in with the thickening layer of leaves; but—with each new leaf that fell—the leaves tugged with invisible threads at his gaze and began to worry him a little: once the forest was laid bare and not a single leaf was left on the branches, everything would be visible, exposed to view. Luckily, he thought, soon—as he had discussed in detail with his wife when he'd crept to the house under the cover of darkness one evening and had seen her for the first time after a long while—his hiding place would be ready, and nobody would ever be able to find him there; moved again by the thought of his secret hiding place he began focusing on what was going on below. Now the village, the dozen houses built of roughly hewn fir boards and roofed with shingles, was picture-like in the shimmering mist with men in uniforms coming and going; he saw, as he had for the last few days, that they were searching with their guns at the ready, stabbing their bayonets into the haystacks; his gaze was drawn just then to one particular soldier: he kept his eyes on the man. For a time, as if self-sufficient, the soldier stood stock still in the yard and then went into the house; he winced, with his hand moving toward his gun quicker than thought, so he couldn't be sure what he'd really meant to do with his outstretched hand; then between two sharpened glances at the village he wondered if she—his Drenka—had been faithful to him all through the war. He remembered straightaway that this was why he'd married her, because he knew she would never betray him, cheat on him: he always saw that in her eyes, ever since the first time he'd caught sight of her, when they were dancing in a circle and with their eyes

11

they sent each other smiles; the soldier left the house quickly, went into the barn, then appeared again and twice stomped his boots. Another two men appeared from somewhere in the yard, in dark overcoats with capes flung over them: their long and sharp bayonets affixed to their guns shone as if they'd gathered up all the light of the day; they walked around, there they were between haystacks, then gone, going in and out of the houses; he lay where he was and watched their every move.

As the strong sunbeams scattered ever more widely through the forest, he remembered that he ought to put away everything metal that might glimmer in the light: first, lying on his side and twisting his body left–right, he stripped off the jacket of his uniform, stowed it in his pack, where there were still some rifle rounds and a folding pocket razor—he ran his hand over his week-old stubble and thought that soon he ought to shave. He loosened, pulled off and slowly worked into his pack the leather belt with the pistol in the holster, which he had stripped from a dead fellow fighter in the early days of the war. He stretched out, went on watching, anticipating that by taking up a new angle he'd shift away from the thought of how, as more leaves fell, they'd spot him and then, right there in front of everybody in the village—in front of his family, wife, children—they'd shoot him! The soldiers down there were gone without a trace, out of sight, so as if toasting to that, he took the canteen, and while keeping an eye on the village and leaning back, he swigged several long gulps of water that had gone tepid in the sun.

He shifted slowly over onto the other elbow and again trained his eyes on his house, and when two little boys suddenly entered his field of vision, followed by his wife in a broad, black skirt (her brother was recently killed in a skirmish at Pasji Vrh), he inadvertently shifted position; everything he saw at that moment, as always when he watched them from here, he wanted to hold onto inside him; from the long wire strung in the plum orchard behind the house his wife was taking down the white laundry, the boys, roughly the same height, ran around the house and shouted loudly over one another. As soon as his wife filled the trough with the washing, she raised it to her shoulder, summoned the boys; they came running right over; for a moment it looked as if his wife and boys were carrying the body of a dead person into the house; with a swift shudder he dispelled the grim thought. He looked more closely at the boys; his wife walked behind them and called something to them he couldn't hear. She was probably, he thought, warning them to watch out for the high threshold to the house, over which he had tripped a few times as a child, fallen, skinned his knees, and once over that threshold he'd also bashed in his nose. After the yard was empty again and all that was left in it were the fat shadows of the house and the linden tree that grew next to it, he felt in his chest the ache of isolation: in everything around him he felt the presence of this isolation, in the leaves, the trees, the clouds, a fly buzzing again around his head, making tangled crazy eights as if sending secret signals, so with a quick swat of the hand he squished it on his shoulder.

He lay on the blanket that had over the last days soaked up the smell of rotten leaves and damp earth: under his thick brows he spent most of his time watching the village, then the mixed canopy above his head, noticing all the while how the colors were fading. Sometimes out of the corner of his eye he'd peek at the gleaming orb of the sun, gauging the time of day; never had time passed more slowly: he kept lying there in that one spot, sensing in his nose the sharp odor of melting resin, and all that was moving around him began to bother him: the sun, the wind, the birds that often flew low with their winged sounds over the forest.

When the afternoon sun finally set behind dark clouds, he took his rifle, pressed the walnut-wood butt up against his right shoulder, and peered at the village through the sights; there they were again, searching, speaking with villagers—he kept them in his sights the whole time; on his fingertip he felt the pulse of the trigger, he did not think to shoot, that would be plain foolishness, but in this way, by attuning his body through the rifle sights, the time passed more readily. In the early evening he sharpened his ears even more; he was glad because he knew that any minute now she'd be there, bringing him news, food, water. He harkened through the silence and twilight to her footsteps, he could tell them apart from among thousands of other steps; she walked as warily as a doe, paused as if stopping to think about something, then suddenly moved ahead. He could hardly wait to hug her, and what if the children came, too? But, he thought, better they still know nothing; he'd see them when the time came.

She emerged slowly from the bushes; on her feet she wore sheepskin slippers, and over her simple black dress she'd flung a shepherd's bag with blue and red tassels. She turned briefly, a quick sigh ran through her body; she came over to him, dropped to her bare knees and then whispered through an intake of breath, "I'm here," and immediately began pulling from her little bag a hunk of bread, crunchy and yellow like the sun that had just set beyond the hill, a slab of cheese, two peeled boiled eggs, and a wicker demijohn of water plugged with a piece of corn cob. "Do you three have enough?" he asked. "Don't let them go hungry." She shook her head, and, still shaking it, whispered, "They've never gone hungry." He nodded and began to eat, trying with his fingers to cram as much as possible into his mouth. "How's it down there?" he chewed, examining the heel of the bread in his hand, and without waiting for an answer he reached for the canteen, shook several drops from it onto the ground, then poured in fresh water and began drinking, guzzling and chasing the food down with it. The woman took a deep breath and said, filling the cracks between her words with quick sighs, "They're looking for you, every day they're looking for you, they've dug up the whole village." He shook the demijohn a few times for no particular reason and said, "They can shake salt on my tail." Again he sipped, screwed the plug onto the canteen as his wife plucked a dry burr from his sleeve and almost inaudibly, in a voice woven now of many voices, as if she weren't the only one wondering this, said, "So I was thinking you turn yourself in and tell them you didn't do nothing wrong." He first wiped his wet mouth with his hand, coughed, listening to her hushed breathing, then, with a glance at the village that knit his brows briefly together, said, "I'll turn myself in when the time comes, not when they say so!" In the end, once he'd eaten everything, he ran the tips of his fingers through the grass to find the crumbs of the bread and cheese, tossed them greedily into his mouth; he moved closer to his wife, pulled her to him, smoothed the hair tied back in her black ponytail that fell down her sturdy back; for a time he leaned his head, resting, against hers, feeling down the line of his spine a strange relief, like when, as a boy, he'd kept watch over their flock in the forest with his mother—he'd lay his head in her lap and with her fingers she'd pick through his hair, searching for lice. "I'll turn myself in within two or three months, not right away while the blood's still boiling," he said, straightened up into a sitting position and pouring more water from the demijohn into the canteen. "So you're off then?" He plugged the demijohn, and then the canteen swiftly as well. "A little longer," she said, and he repeated her words to himself. "Mijo," she added, "do you think this all will end well?" "Can't end any way but well," he said, shifting his body to a new position, and he looked high above her head at the gloaming forest, as if signaling to her that she ought to be making her way back. She suddenly hugged him and pressed close. "Now, off you go," he stroked her back and lay slowly down by his rifle, "and look after those boys," he said, noticing how at the word "boys" something caught in his throat.

When she'd disappeared completely from view, slipping from tree to tree like a shadow, he began to think about what he'd say, one day, if he were to turn himself in (he closed his eyes so he could think about this more easily); he'd tell them without holding back how everything had happened, that it all began with the celebration, when the speaker in his top hat got up on the stage in the small town of G. (he was seeing a hat like that for the first time) and said (he still remembered the man's three hoarse declarations), "Anybody who threatens the survival of our country will be put to death"; then "They are threatening our future"; and in the end (and this he wouldn't tell them) "Communism, that's when a brother fucks his sister." If they think he's guilty for believing this learned man—and he thinks he isn't, because he never slaughtered nor killed, except maybe when he shot at those who were shooting at him, but that was war, and in war there is shooting—they can go ahead, if they choose, to judge him fairly, and he will do his time; just so he's able to return to his

wife and children as soon as possible; to his mea-
ger soil, because he has none better; he shifted
from lying down to sitting, and then abruptly he
looked up, unsure of what he was looking for: full
of restlessness, he began pulling on his army coat
to keep from thinking about anything; absent-
mindedly he did up the single-breasted row of
brass buttons from bottom to top, barely able to
do them up properly: in the end he straightened
the collar on his army shirt; he was suddenly
swept into a fine mood by an image—his axe over
his shoulder and his tall, square-shouldered sons
walking behind him, singing brightly—and began
to breathe more calmly. Oh, everything will be
fine. He stared at his muddy sleeve, having made
his peace with an armored beetle that had been
scuttling around on it—he could just as easily
make his peace with those he'd fought against
during the war—and thought that the day would
come when he'd tell his grandsons about all this
around a campfire.

The night was still full of moonlight, he picked
up his rifle and stretched out his legs; the round
moon like an all-seeing eye followed his wary

steps: he knew the terrain well, all the paths, even the smallest tracks through the forest, every tree, every boulder. Here as a boy he had tended cattle for years. He stepped out onto the meadow, for a time he skirted hazelnut shrubs, replete with a nighttime freshness, and picked hazelnuts. For two hours or so he roamed through the thicket, broke off clusters of hazelnuts, then, his pockets bulging with the nuts, he turned to go back. He didn't pass by a single tree without giving it a close look; each tree seemed poised to come alive at any moment and grab him by the neck. When—still feeling on his back the gaze of the many-eyed forest—he returned hastily to his lair, he wrapped himself in his blanket, raised his collar, listening in the distance to the rattle of gunfire and the hoot of an owl that further congealed the dark. The guns stilled, but thunder began, and lightning struck somewhere deep in the forest; he worried about rain: he'd find the coming days harder to endure soaking wet; he'd have to seek shelter in a nearby cave, but he couldn't be sure they weren't searching it daily; everybody, even the smallest of children around here, knew about that cave. He positioned the rifle next to him and thought about where he'd leave it when he went down into his hiding place: down there, he thought, the pistol with a full chamber would be enough, the rifle would only get in the way. Lightning was still flashing: light and dark alternated in the one view.

In the morning, groggy from sleep, he was awakened by the song of birds; to his right he heard shepherds noisily driving their sheep out to pasture, their voices hoarse from constant shouting, then the sounds of the whetting of a scythe, quick, growing louder; to his left along the nearby forest path someone's oxen were hauling a cart with iron-rimmed wooden wheels; they ground the rocks under them. Then somewhere from these sounds, rather than from his own head, came a memory of his late father; once with oxen along this same rutted path full of sharp rocks, his mother, father, and he were driving a cart with a load of beech logs, and Mrkonja's hoof was so gashed that his father took off both his own wool socks and put them on the ox to cover the painful, lame back hoof.

While he nibbled slowly at the hazelnuts in his hand, his attention was drawn to the intermittent clatter of machine-gun fire: it came from across the village, beyond the belly of the bare mountain whose pale peak could always just barely be discerned, even in daylight; he cracked open the hazelnuts with his teeth and scanned the village: there were no soldiers cruising through it daily now, though, hand on heart, they might turn up at any time. He was worried they might start nosing around in the forest near the village—he believed this, too, would happen soon enough; he looked up at the dome of the sky: gray clouds were again threatening rain; lightning flashed several times, blazing stripes went chasing one after another every so often across the sky. Then everything suddenly, again, hushed. Only a sparrow hawk angled across the firmament, sharp against the sky, as if it didn't dare bring its flight to an end; he watched the hawk and with a deep sigh he thought, *Ah, friend, if I had your wings.* Then, pleased and grateful, he looked up at the sky that had been merciful with the weather for days and under his breath, said, "So no rain yet."

From his viewpoint, the sky was entirely at a slant, if only he could somehow chase time faster down that slope. He munched on the hazelnuts, spat out the shells, and between each mouthful time spooled again; a fresh stare fixed on the skinny branches, the thinning leaves in constant motion as if unsure of whether to stay or fall, and then one leaf that had fluttered down and left behind it a bared branch—all this stirred anger in him at his wife. "What the fuck is she still waiting for!" he said to himself. Once he'd regained his composure, he studied the flight of a bee that buzzed around the hat-shaped blossoms; then he watched a bird that first chirped on a branch then flew to the ground and sharpened its yellow beak on a stone, then the calyx of a flower in which the sun blazed—as if this were the point from which, at any moment, a new day would be born. After a time, everything in the world, even his heart, seemed to have stopped moving. He lay and for hours he filled the emptiness of the day with his gaze. Then he began to fix on a silken Hymenoptera that flew alone in circles around itself, as if borne more by the wind than by its will; he lightly touched his thumb to a grasshopper and it leaped so far that it defied all the laws of nature, and this, again, unnerved him; because, how could an insect possibly do such a thing, yet a person could not? He closed his eyes and began recognizing the sounds around him only by distant memory; then several times he angrily smacked his hand down on the thick litter of leaves, and each time a bird—with a sound like the noise of a curtain being drawn—was flushed from the bushes; his eye was grazed by a quick little midge though he hadn't even noticed when it flew in; he pressed his hand across both eyes and an image instantly merged and flipped: he saw himself, his wife, children, as they all sat happily around the table, husking beans from dried pods; just as he had done years ago with his parents.

With his eyes closed he kept shifting position; he turned, twitched, tightened the muscles in his arms, legs, face. He had closed his eyes because this way he saw so much more clearly (nothing could escape his memory), he fingered the leaves, crumbled them; in his head was the rattle of grain yet there was no grain in the fields; above his head trees bent over him with no color and full of sad sighs, as if sympathetic; then, with a quick glance, he linked the distant echo of a cannon to the shriek of a bird that flapped above him; he rolled over onto his back, tucked his hands under his head, stared into the distant, foggy heights. He kept company with the newly multiplied shrieks of spiky birds that flew out from the bare treetops, flew up and down (each with its own trajectory), left and right, as if bent on measuring the sky; now, when he felt he might be feverish though luckily he was not (he touched his forehead), everything around him seemed too fast again; the sky caved into the heights; the wind howled and quickly forgot all that surrounded it; with trepidation, listening to the savage roar, he thought that in a matter of days, or hours, or minutes, his children would have grown up, becoming men he would no longer know.

He did a double take (he still couldn't believe it), and his Adam's apple played on his throat; he peered at the broad, white sheet hanging over the fence of dry stakes—the agreed-upon signal—and then with his rifle and pack on his back he crawled to a nearby rocky patch, found a largish crevice, pushed the rifle and the rounds in, and then piled grass, soil, rocks, and ferns over the craggy niche in whichever order each came to hand. He returned and waited for nightfall; he would have no difficulty, he thought, making his way unnoticed down the slope to his house and crawling into the hiding place. Why, he could even go right now, if he felt brash enough, he could tear off branches, use them as camouflage and dash across the clearing, but he was unwilling to take the risk. There were no soldiers, but there were people in the village who, eager to ingratiate themselves with the new authorities, might turn him in: there have always, he thought, been folks among us who, when they look in the mirror, see two faces.

When day pulled silently away from night and the heavens broke out in countless stars— before the dark had settled fully upon the forest edge—he buckled on the pistol belt, cinched it tightly, tossed his knapsack over his shoulder. He smoothed the dip where he'd lain on the ground, kicking leaves over it, straightened up, and did something he'd done many years before, while still a boy: he clasped his hands and said, aloud,

"God help me." Earlier he had done this, too, like
the last time when he was breaking through an
encirclement in combat and called upon God, but
his hands—not since he was little had he clasped
his hands so fervently. He set out following a
path cut deeply through the grass, then warily,
sideways, descended the earthen steps (they were
also boundaries), along which the grassy slope
fell away toward the village; he strode down the
bulging furrows full of nighttime hush; he walked
with his head bowed low as if on the lookout for
something and gradually adapted his steps to the
firmness of the soil; in each new step he felt there
to be something final. Not a single dog in the
village barked, as if they were conspiring; on he
walked and in the brisker night air he picked up
the fragrance of the barn; yes, for him this was
always fragrance, never an odor , just as the lilacs
in spring, young clover, dry hay were fragrances,
and each time during the years of war he'd come
across fresh dung, still steaming, he'd close his
eyes and nothing could take him faster to the
bosom of his home than that fragrance. It didn't
take him long, with rapid steps, head bowed, to
trot to the linden tree; for a few moments, full

of a closely held tension, he stood locked onto the tree bark, scribbled with old-age cracks, then he gazed up into the dark canopy of the giant. Rising on his tiptoes, he looked around and then strode to the front of the house and hid along the wooden wall, under the bundles of shucked corn cobs that hung from it and brushed his head tenderly; he held his breath to hear better; his heart pounded; he looked toward the window into the yellow flickering light of the kerosene lamp: shadows played across the ceiling from the chipped cylinder and he knew every crack in it; ringing voices came from the house, the clatter of dishes; then he straightened, tore himself abruptly away from the spot and ran silently to the latched barn door: he took care to be sure that the hinges didn't creak in their pins.

He slipped in among the walls that were coated in darkness, among the warm cattle: all were standing and watching him, their eyes wide; only stirring were the chickens—housed behind a wooden partition—that began flapping their wings in fear, but, he thought, at least his wife upstairs will know he'd finally arrived; he closed the door slowly behind him, patted the oxen; both had white vertical stripes from their brows to their red muzzles; he sat on the wooden trough between the oxen, stroking them over their smooth, taut skin, and reached under the neck of one to the dappled cow. "How are you?" he said with a lilt in his voice and a throat full of excitement, releasing with each new breath the tension in his body. The cattle—even before he'd made a sound—recognized him, they twisted their necks toward him, bathed him with warm steam from their wide nostrils, tried to catch him with their rough tongues, so, grinning, he had to fend them off with his elbows to keep them from licking his face and hair; the chickens kept up their clucking, but soon they, too, simmered down; he felt a joyous thrill that he was here in his barn, in his own home, with his cattle, here, right underneath his wife and children, and for a moment he was moved by this elation to break into song, to hold on to the welling of happiness inside him for as long as he could. Up above, overhead, the children were scampering about, giggling, the boards creaked and moved, so his thought of singing was bumped out by a new thought of moving somewhere safe as soon as possible.

He listened to the cascade of urine that streamed from the cow onto the packed dirt, and as he was preparing to leave, he suddenly rolled up his sleeves instead and, with the moon peering into the barn, took the pitchfork from behind the door and began mucking out the stalls: he lumped the dung together with the tines; carefully shaped the doughy mass, rolled it, and forked in damp straw from each side until fully blended, speared the mass on the tines of the fork, and, with measured swings (how much barn dung had he thrown out that little window), he heaved it onto the muck heap outside against the wall. Whenever he threw the dung, he always took special care not to harm the cattle, as a boy he'd feared this most of all: the cattle might suddenly shift position and he'd stab them with the pitchfork. He scooped armfuls of fresh straw from the corner and spread them evenly under the cattle, and then from a conical mound in the same corner he grabbed two or three handfuls of sawdust and sprinkled it through his fingers under the cattle's hooves to keep them as dry as possible for sleeping. Finally, he took an armful of hay from a basket woven of willow twigs and divided it fairly along the trough: while he worked, giving himself totally over to his rapid movements, he forgot about the war and the people out to catch him, as if this were the most ordinary day and he'd walk out of the barn and go upstairs to the house with his children and wife to eat dinner in peace.

He stood there motionless a while longer, watching the cattle as they chewed with relish, angling toward the trough; he went out and closed the door soundlessly behind him. He took a cautious look all around: from somewhere someone's dog was likely to bark; for years he hadn't had a dog. A warm wind blew from behind the house and the tops of the trees—their long branches mingling—rustled with the leaves they still had left, as if transmitting messages at a whisper that nobody else should hear, about how after such a long time he had at last come home. Still followed by the moon's gaze full of nocturnal secrets and a breeze that pleasantly caressed his face, he turned, head bowed, toward the heap of firmly packed barn muck that was still radiating the warmth of the day, shifting his weight slowly from one foot to the other; he leaned over a little more and warily moved aside a length of rotten board that had been smeared on all sides with a thick and now dried layer of dark manure: behind it there was a round, narrow opening, blacker than the night itself, enveloping him on all sides. For a time he stood there, motionless, beside the heap, which looked like a smaller shadow of the barn, and beyond it he watched his house lit by the distinct, yellow window, cutting sharply into the dark; but he was no longer capable of thinking of anything else, he just stared motionless at the stars and the moon, as if only with them did he wish to exchange the occasional thought. Then, with a single movement, he crept slowly in on all fours and covered the entrance with the board, using both hands to fix it carefully in place, snuffing the last rays of moonlight.

In the dark, through a half-breath he wiped his hands, no longer visible, on his pantlegs and hugged his head to his knees; the heavy stench prevented him from thinking clearly about any-thing, about how this was now his destiny, his salvation, and when he first set foot outside of his hiding place, a different world would be out there where enemies would no longer be enemies and he would no longer be somebody on the run: all would be as if he'd been born again; the one clear and pure thought—and with it the stink little by little thinned in his nose—was that what mattered most now was to get some sleep. Soon, surrounded by his sense of safety and warmth that grew with each new thought of all the nice things that would come one day, once he was free, he curled up in a fetal position, closed his eyes, and dropped off to sleep.

Dogs

1935

THE ROOSTER CROWED; THE SUN PEERED OUT
from behind the jagged wall of the woods, entered
the room, and was snared in a spiderweb; he
watched the glow through the mesh of the web,
and then he spotted a bird of prey flying over the
village, on the lookout for something to anchor
it. "Mother," he shouted, "where're the chickens?"
He heard the reedy, shrill voice: "Here with me!"

He came out of the house, went to the well, lowered into it a wooden bucket attached to a chain,
and after it sank in, he drew it up with several
sharp pulls, set it on the rim, splashed himself
with water under his rancid armpits. "Watch that
hawk!" he called. He doused the nape of his neck,
his chest, and his face, red with the frigid water
of the well, went back into the house that was
covered in wooden patches: the light overtook

him for a moment, but he squashed it with the rickety door. He sat on a chair and, crooking his elbow, rapidly shoveled in spoonfuls of the bread crumbled into milk that his mother had left for him on the table that morning: he glanced out the window, eyeing the sparrow hawk that had perched on a tall linden, and then, after Mother's sharpened cry, it shrieked, *kverrrr, kverrrr*—the chickens huddling, frightened, around her—and off it winged with wild flaps. "There's a bullet waiting for you!" he hollered after it, though he didn't know what he'd have to shoot it with, except their old musket, handmade, more of a danger for the person doing the shooting than for whoever was at the receiving end of the shot.

He returned inside to pull on a homespun shirt before stepping back out into the yard to look for his mother. All in black, a triangular kerchief on her head and eyes set deep under her brows, she was kneeling and gathering nettles in a sack; she snatched at them swiftly to keep from being stung, like when she put a red ember back into the ravenous cast-iron stove with her bare hands. "Where's Papa gone?" he asked and in passing patted the young dog that was emerging slowly from the hollowed trunk of a beech. "Over to Josa's to sharpen the hoe." He gave her a nod and went to the battered stump, pulled out the axe, planted it on his shoulder, and said, unaware that he was using his father's raspy voice, "I'm off to the woods to take down those trees and I'll be dragging one home." He turned with the axe on his shoulder and looked at the meadow where children, with their bowl-cut hair, were running around an ever-pregnant woman, chasing after a fly that was giving a name to each thing it landed on; the boys were racing around it in a frenzy, shouting, "There's the fly on the horns! There's the fly on that rake!" "Oh, my Mijo," said his mother, looking over the fence at the romping children, "better get yourself a girl; him and me—we're not good for much, and we won't be around much longer." He ran the edge of his thumb along the blade of the axe and said, "I'm off!"

He leaned over and, with the sun on his back, rolled his pants up, running his hand down his muscular calves that swelled with raw strength, then with axe in hand he set off across the freshly mown meadow dotted with old molehills. As he walked he kicked apart the molehills. He saw a plowman and passed a boy—the seat of his pants covered in patches—who, with a curly-haired, panting dog, was herding a flock of sheep toward the woods while playing a double flute; he greeted the boy with a nod. The boy waved back and went on puffing vigorously into the flute. Supported by the wind, Mijo began whistling the boy's tune, then to sing it: "Oh, bear, you mountain beast, who is there to scratch you, who will wash you..."

By a wild cherry tree he stood and cocked his ear to the noise of the black fruit, ripening: he pulled off a cherry, downed it (bursting in his mouth), spat out the pit, stomped on it, and walked on to the nearby woods: the pathway was winding, alive with bugs, and each step along the path, over-grown in grasses, made the difference for them between life and death.

As soon as he entered the woods he set down his axe in the grass and shinnied up the tallest tree, where he had the perfect view; he'd climbed here as a boy when he wanted to see the world—because

while you were on your way up there didn't seem
to be much of a difference between the sky and
the ground, but once you reached the very top…
the sky was farther away than you could possibly imagine. The fresh air sped his movements;
he wanted as soon as possible to see where she
was with her sheep. He wedged himself in firmly
between forking branches, hugged the tree, and
craned his neck to search among the green flanks
of the meadows; once more he slowly circled his
head around, gazing over at the neighboring village where Drenka was from, on whose hilltop
stood a church with those many-colored windows
made of the very finest bits of sunlight that even
now were gleaming, and next to the church the
upright poplars stood on guard: he heard a brief
noise and looked down: through the leaves ran
a deer, it froze, he regretted that he didn't have
his axe in hand. A branch crunched underfoot
and the deer jumped back, confused, with its eye
attuned to the source of the sound, then on it
went, loping, alive only while it ran. Mijo came
down slowly and when he was still a meter off the
ground he jumped and landed spryly on both feet;
he quickly took the axe, making up for lost time,

swung and began chopping at the foot of another tree with the sharp blade, shaking the red leaves from it—for some ten minutes he chopped without pause, always with the same, steady strokes, breathing through the cracks in the air: every blow had its own special sound, until the tree, human-like, bowed low exuding the dense smell of heartwood. Then Mijo pushed it with both hands and it snapped and crashed down onto the other trees, which held it up, wounded. Mijo chopped once more, severing it from its trunk, grabbed it, and pulled it from the forest's embrace onto open ground; he trimmed it with well-aimed strokes and sat, victorious, upon it. Then he pulled his wet shirt up over his head, jumped to his feet again, grabbed his axe, and pounced on the other trees, until one by one, he'd chopped down five of them and trimmed them to perfection.

He climbed back up to the crown in the canopy (quickly making his way skyward), found a spot by the top, and, tightly hugging the tree, looked around, but again across his broad field of vision he did not catch sight of her nor hear the tinkle of bells; with furrowed brow he let loose his thoughts: maybe she'd already come and gone and would be back tomorrow. He spotted a dark figure in the distance on a bicycle whom he recognized at once, he was the man with the drum, the drum he'd beat with sticks and announce, "Hear ye, hear ye! Hear ye..." He climbed down and then he could hear the rhythmic beat of the drum, mixing with the barking of dogs. He tied his shirt around his waist and grabbed a downed tree, taking his axe in his other hand and—wondering about taxes and the tax collector—he dragged the tree behind him toward the village. While he was walking, bent forward at a slant, the trees around him leaned one on the next, lending everything the illusion of a slope, and this made him feel even more tired; every time he stopped to rest a little, he'd hear the beating of the drum (pellets of sound), like pattering grain pouring somewhere nearby; then a dry breeze began blowing from the woods, much stronger, charging through the trees, and every time the drumbeat was heard, the wind distorted it beyond recognition: he sped up his pace and traversed grass laid low by the heat, eager to hear the news brought by the crier.

He dropped the axe and tree by the house (peo-ple had already slowly begun dispersing), went indoors, hastily pulled on another shirt, and went to his father who was standing, motionless, in the middle of the village. He inquired with a thrust of the chin. His father answered, "Over by Letinac a dog bit a constable so now they've banned us from keeping dogs." Mijo half-turned and watched the man with the drum walk to his bicycle; the man stopped and lifted his foot the way a horse's hoof is lifted when it's being shod; the man poked at it with his fingers, prying pebbles loose from the raised ridges of his tall boots, then sat on the bicycle and rode slowly off; while he cycled down the road, raising dust and spinning the pedals faster and faster in a taut arc—shrinking to the size of a bug—an old woman hollered after him, "Be your seed forever cursed!"

At dawn his father was mowing the meadow; his body hunched, his head still, as if it weren't part of his scrawny, twisted frame, and his inner thoughts found a voice in the constant hiss of the scythe: to shave the face of the earth in as broad a swath as possible.

Leaning on an apple tree that had borne no fruit, Mijo watched his father, his sunburned neck: when he paused for a moment to whet the scythe, his wrinkled face hovered above the grass. As he paused, his gaze lagged behind all else that was happening, seeing nothing but the black whetstone that slid, easy and natural, left–right, over the metal. Stepping gingerly, one foot after the other, Mijo evaded the rooster with its yellow, fleshy spurs, careful not to brush it with his foot; he made his way slowly over to his father and waited for a pause in the sharpening. "Let me!" he said. His father bent down, grabbed a fistful of fresh grass, used it to wipe smooth the blade of the scythe, and, squinting through particles of sunlight, he said, "Here, take some of this grass to the cow." Mijo crouched, gathered up an armful of the fragrant grass, and the cow began lowing and trumpeting from in the barn; Mijo quickly delivered her fodder to the cramped space, set it before her in the wooden trough; she was still lying down, her belly bulging. Then slowly, full of care for the calf she was carrying, she clambered up onto her legs; he stood, looked at her round belly, listening to how his father was working, lying on the ground, at the peening anvil; Mijo peered out and saw him sheltered by the linden, one leg slightly raised, the other out straight, hammering away with the precision of a watchmaker along the blade of the scythe, thinning it to razor sharpness; his father worked it tirelessly with a steady intensity, as if the sound of the hammering was now permanent, teasing the harsh ring from the scythe, but the shadow of the hand he was hammering with, as though he and the scythe were one, fled from him and jarred the harmony.

Mijo returned to the cow, from a nail driven into the wooden wall he took a steel comb and began running it over her shining red hairs (much more gently over her belly), which grew shinier with each stroke; the cow turned her head to look at him with her big, gleaming eyes and you could tell she was enjoying this, a few times she swatted him out of affection across his back with her tail; in the end he pulled the hairs off the comb, wadded them up into a ball, and tossed them through the little window, below which was the piled mound of barn muck. He heard his mother calling him to lunch.

Father was already seated at the table; he coughed, and his cough shook the house to its foundations. Mijo sat across from him, waiting for Mother to put the pot with beans on the table. She filled their bowls up to the brim (her dented one only half-way). Through the window came the sun, gathered in a sheaf of thick, yellow light; they ate in silence, Mijo forced himself, between his short breaths, to eat more slowly, but he had trouble, because he'd acquired the habit of eating speedily while he was still a boy, when he wrangled with his sisters over every bite of food on the table. Father ate slowly, but at times he, too, would speed up because he had also fought with his sisters and brothers over mouthfuls, and he still had a scar under his left eye from one such fight when he'd grabbed a potato from the hands of his younger brother, and his brother nearly gouged his eye out with a fork; Mijo once grabbed his older sister by the hair because on Christmas Eve she snatched a piece of meat from the tip of his knife, and he held on until a lock of her hair was left in his hand—though his father was beating him wildly on the back with the hollow bone of a gnawed beef shank from which he'd just sucked the marrow.

The dog barked outside, Father winced, and to the cooling pool of bean stew in front of him he said, "Take it as soon as you can." Mijo looked out the window toward the woods and, shifting on the uncomfortable chair, said, "Wouldn't it be better if Mile took his gun and…" Father began scooping the beans up with his spoon, and afterward he wiped his whole plate clean with bread. "And who will pay him for that bullet?" he said. Mother stood up, cleared the plates, and pushed them into a bucket of water. "The pup's a young one, it's shame," she said. "Yes, it's young, but the constables will come and take our cow and the calf inside her." He stood up, resting his fists on the tabletop, sighing deeply, and coughing again into his right hand. Mijo said, "What about the old musket?" Father said, "Forget all that." "But if we're being fair," said Mother and looked out the window, "never have we had a worse dog in this house. Every fox can waltz right past it and steal our chickens." The cow mooed beyond the partition, Father gave another deep cough, sipped water from a small pot, and muttered, "I'll be off to see to her, could be she's thirsty." Mijo went out into the yard after his father and watched him go through the other, worm-eaten door to the cow, prattling to her. Mijo went to the little wooden doghouse, around which pranced a scrawny black dog, merrily wagging its tail stump; when his father brought it home in his arms a year before, he chopped its tail off right away on the chopping block so it would bark and growl more: that was the usual fate of dogs in their village, but Father later said, "Even chopping off three tails wouldn't have made it any fiercer."

Mijo pressed the pup firmly between his legs, ran his hands along the right and left keyboards of its ribs, and shook a cold boiled potato out of his pocket: the dog gobbled up the potato, reared up on its hind legs, and sniffed at Mijo's right pocket. The hawk appeared again and sank vertically and slowly from the sky, its body lazy though its gaze was swift and decisive. Mother shouted, "pi, pi," from the house, and a few chickens and the rooster found themselves just then out in the middle of the yard. Then Father came out, coughed, took up the birch broom, and began sweeping leaves, mingling with the lengthened shadow of the hawk.

Again he ran his hand along the dog's spine, and when he started off with it on a loose chain, Mother said, "Take note after you tie it up, so you know where to go back and fetch the chain from." He nodded, raked his fingers through his tangled hair, and set off; he walked along slowly and the dog kept up with him like a shadow. In the village a dog suddenly barked, another dog romped around the field after a bird, and then a shot was heard, as if a dry tree had snapped, then the whimpering of the dog and then another muted shot, after which all went quiet. Mijo and the dog were already at the first steep clearing above the village; he went on walking until the dog stopped to scratch itself behind the ear. Mijo pulled it along after him, saying, "Come on," the dog scampered quickly but then slowed and shortened its steps. Mijo sped steadily up for several hundred meters, and when he sat to rest, the dog stood behind him, its heavy tongue hanging out and its sides shivering rhythmically. "You're already tuckered out," he told it; he held off from patting it because that way the parting would be harder for the dog and for him; he didn't even want to look at it, so the dog wouldn't spot in his eyes what was on his mind.

There was a tinkling of bells. He listened once more, trapped in a single beat of his heart, and then he set off much faster with the dog over the craggy bosom of the land, until he'd crossed the clearing they'd always called the dell, then up a hillside of old charred stumps, where the bells could be heard more clearly, in the rhythm the sheep used to work their jaws. He waded into the dense undergrowth. Next to a bush he saw a girl he knew: she was sitting on her sweater with her legs tucked under her, passing the time by picking at the leather slipper on her foot. Right next to his eye he noticed a spider that was weaving from the silence its shivering web between two leafing branches and had caught its reflection in a mirror-like droplet of water, measuring its beauty; he went back across the rocks, tied the dog to a tree, and indicated silence with a finger to his lips; as if it fully understood, the dog first sat, then laid its head on the ground, crossed its muzzle with its black paws, and closed its eyes. Mijo stretched out, peered through the bushes. Picking a dry stick up from the ground, he muttered something, and when he swiftly broke the stick over his raised knee the girl sat up. Over his knee again, Mijo broke the shorter half of the stick, which now snapped louder yet, and he could see the pale face of the girl, laughing, and her black hair looking blacker still. Mijo stepped out from among the trees, hopped over a white rock criss-crossed with veins of sunlight, and the girl sat back down, smiling, in the grass. Mijo said, "Hand me a little water." She passed him her demijohn, he took out the plug of black tow, drank a few sips, and said, letting the words ripen in his mouth, "Ah, you saved me." The girl got up, went over on her slender white ankles to the sheep, and, waving her arms, chased one of them that had wandered off from the flock to nibble at a bush, driving it back to the huddled herd. "So, where's your dog, Šarko?" asked Mijo when she came back and sat down next to him, her knees pressed firmly together. "Where can Šarko be?" she said, turning a small stone between her fingers as if counting prayer beads: "Yesterday Poppa..." Mijo rolled a dry hazelnut out of his pocket, bit into it, extracted the nut to hand to her, but she shook her head. Mijo threw the nut high above his head and then caught it neatly in his mouth, pulverizing it with little nips of his teeth. He jumped up, went teetering across the rocks to the bushes with his arms widespread as if tightrope-walking across the heights, picking a few more hazelnuts: "They sure had a good year." He sat even closer to her, so he nudged her foot with his, she nudged back with hers. She jumped up suddenly, spat out a flower she'd been chewing on, opened her palm in front of her, and declared, "Rain!" "What rain?" said Mijo calmly, raising his head, he studied the dark, taut membrane of the sky. "There, a drop fell on my hand," she said and showed him her wet palm: a drop fell on the girl's brow, and a second on Mijo's nose. The girl picked her sweater up off the ground, tied it snugly around her waist, grabbed her cloth bag, tossed it over her shoulder, and said, "I'll be off, otherwise I'll get wet." "Sit a little longer," said Mijo, "you're not made of sugar." But she was already dashing off. Mijo jumped up and called after her, "Have you seen Drenka?" As she ran she shook her head, but he wasn't sure whether she was saying yes or no, and then on she ran after her sheep.

From somewhere came a buzzing hum, and right behind it a sluggish bumblebee, barely keeping up with its droning sound. Again Mijo glanced at the low sky, where the clouds were black, piling up, so he went over to the dog, undid the chain, and set off through the play of light. The sun peeked again from behind a cloud—now you see me, now you don't—toying with those who were keeping track of it.

Mijo walked, marking the way under his feet with his eyes. Up the taut chain, through every link, he felt the dog's quickened breath: but still, this way is better, he thought—looking back at the pup over his shoulder then quickly shaking off its doggy gaze—than tying a rope around its neck and casting it into a bottomless pit, the way many in the village would do it over the next few days; if he had to shoot it himself with the musket that would be so much worse, then he'd have to look it in the eye because how else would he be able to hit its head without looking it in the eye, and no way did he want to wound it and then have to shoot it again—having to measure the gunpowder out from the horn again, insert another musket ball, tamp the bore, insert the paper plug, then tamp it again while listening to the yowls of the wounded dog. While swinging with his free arm to the rhythm of his steps, always a chain length ahead, he passed through curtains of silence. He twisted his tongue in his mouth and a few times he whistled boldly, because the silence of the forest always unnerved him, and the dog, while pulling its paws from the noose of the wiry grass, yipped at the birds that fluttered from the branches.

When he arrived at the woodland full of younger trees, he pulled out his knife and on the soft bark of a green tree, at eye height, he carved her name. Coasting on the sound of the wind he stared at the white, uneven letters from which oozed the thick sap. He closed his eyes, and saw her again running to meet him, her braids lit by the sun like long candles. Meanwhile the dog flopped down again, as if it had spent all its energy yipping at the birds, so Mijo had to tug at it to come along after him: they walked, one behind the other, and the space between them was filled by the rattling of the chain. Mijo walked on and from time to time thought about the dogs they'd had before: one of them was carried off by a wolf in the forest. It appeared at the forest edge, long, gray (he and Father were chopping down trees with their axes), the mutt barked and the wolf slyly fled, but the mutt took up the chase. They called it to come back, but it ran on after the wolf and never did. A second died of a disease; a third was so vicious that it bit his sister on the hand while she was feeding it so their neighbor Mile had to shoot it; the one before this one—who could have fought a bear—Mother took to the forest because it was old, blind, and had lost all its teeth. Again out of the corner of his eye he stole a glance at the dog that was affectionately rubbing up against his legs; he felt sorry for it, but he was even more sorry for those other ones, who'd been better at guarding the house than this one, better at tending the flock, and who—and again he looked over at it with a pitying glance—were long gone now. But the deeper he went into the forest away from the village and people, the more he felt his bond with the dog, especially when a thought crossed his mind and he uttered it in a low voice to himself: "This dog is mine." His eyes teared up a little, and it surprised him; he thought at once of Drenka and imagined her watching him somewhere from the bushes, and that is how he stemmed the welling tears. He sat, leaning his chin on his joined knees, the dog sat quietly next to him. He dug at the soft soil with the tip of his shoe, but when he thought of the dog's grave, he stopped right away: the arrow-like rain had long since ceased falling, but the forest blackened, and then it grew darker still because the trees where they were passing were full of dark leaves: along the way he and the dog stopped, occasionally, to listen to the silence.

They sped up and crossed a meadow, pressed on all sides by fog, then a stretch of forest so close and inhospitable that each tree was pushing for more room. They arrived at a fir grove, dotted with bushes—a fresh-smelling brook running among them; his breath quickened and with his feelings unclear he firmly chained the dog to a sapling, feeling the rain on his face that was seeking harmony with the burbling water; he closed his eyes, and the healing fluid sound soothed him.

For a time he watched the lively swirl of the water—his gaze ordinary, everything today had to be ordinary. Then in his hair he found a shaft of yellow straw, and through it for a time he sucked at the sharp air, wishing that nothing that was going on around him had anything to do with him. He took his knife, slowly cut through the water course of the little stream, watching how, over its shiny blade, the water flowed and thinking how everything in this world follows a higher order of its own that is beyond his grasp, and this cannot be stopped by anything. With abrupt movements he stood up but then sat back down, not knowing what it was he actually wanted.

A wolf suddenly began to howl: the dog shot up and wholly sharpened its, and thereby Mijo's, ears. From the heart of the dark forest a choir of vulpine voices bayed: they were tuning to each other; the dog went even more rigid, as if every part of its body were a tensed spring. Mijo went over to it, patted its bristling hackles, and said in a voice drawn from a deep shudder, "Little one, don't you be scared now..." It began to whine and Mijo stepped back from the reach of the chain; the dog whined louder and the stump of its tail tried stubbornly to tuck between its back legs as if the whole dog were the quivering stump. As the howls neared the dog began to squeal and yank back as if to uproot the tree: when next it lurched forward, Mijo thrust his fingers deep in his ears. He ran, fell, scrambled up without thinking of anything but getting home as fast as he could. Near the village he finally stopped; around him flashed lightning, snuffing the few stars in the sky. As he went downhill through the yawning dark, he began to bark. The faster he walked, the louder he barked: he felt as if he stopped barking, he'd die.

Celebration

1941

"READY?" CALLED MIJO, STANDING OUT IN FRONT
of the freshly whitewashed stone house fenced
with stakes; he ran his hand over his hair, which
he'd slicked back with sugar water earlier that
morning. Drenka waved to him from the window,
said, "Come in," and then she quickly disappeared
but Mijo went right on staring, silent, motionless,
at the irregular square, expecting her to reappear
so he could send her a secret wink. He adjusted his
blazer that was faded from the sun and the teeth
of time and looked first at the little church with
its copper helmet, then at the row of stakes before
him, then high above the village, at the phalanx
of trees in the greening woodland. Everything
he looked at reminded him of the war that had
just broken out; a dog growled, a dog he hadn't
noticed at first because it lay curled under the
pigsty that had been raised on four smooth rocks,

leaning on the newer end of the house. The door flew open, a man with a wooden crutch stepped out and beckoned him in; with the same swing of his arm the man waved out smoke. "The milk, it boiled over," he said, smiling and taking a greedy gulp of fresh air, then with a wooden hobble of his crutch he went over to the curly-haired dog that barked again, patted it, and said, "It's not long ago we got it and it hasn't yet settled in."

Mijo stepped into the spacious yard, went over to the dog, kneeled, and scratched it between its long, floppy ears, one of which had turned inside out as if to hear them better. "So, what's its name?" asked Mijo. "Garo, they called it," said the man, "but Drenka and Rude, they can give it whatever name they like—I don't care." "I still haven't got a dog, but I'm working on it," said Mijo and looked down at the dog that was rubbing against his leg. The man with the crutch started back to the house and said over his hunched shoulder, "Come on in for a glass of šljivovica, they'll be along soon enough." Mijo ran his hand once more down the dog's back and then gave it a nod as he walked away and entered the house, smelling the pungent odor of burned milk mingling with the light odor of gasoline; on a patch of rag at the end of a long table that was covered in a white tablecloth, there lay a lighter—cube-shaped with a mesh-like casing—that had been taken apart and a knitting needle next to it, the tip charred, and also cotton batting. After trying twice the man managed to lean that crutch of his against the wall; he pulled from the cupboard a flask of brandy and a shot glass, and said, "I can't, but surely you can." He gestured with a thrust of the chin for Mijo to take a seat at the table; Mijo tossed back the first glass, as clear as spring water, but when the man was getting ready to pour him the next, Mijo laid both hands over the glass and, with a nod to the strength of the drink, said, "No more, thank you." "Oh, come now, just one more," said the man. Mijo relented, moving his hands aside; the man poured him the next one and left the uncorked bottle right there beside him. While Mijo was tipping the glass back, slowly this time, a thin young man came down the creaky wooden stairs, his hair dark like Mijo's but wavier, wearing a black suit tailored to measure, and said to Mijo, "So where've you been?"

as he had a quick look at himself in the round mirror hanging on the wall under the slanting wooden stairs. Mijo measured him from behind, head to toe, smiled, and said, "So, Mr. Student, you're gussied up like you're going to a wedding." The boy took a comb, dipped it into the white washbasin full of water, leaned over to see himself better in the mirror, and began slicking back his hair, running the other hand along the wet stripe behind the comb. "This celebration matters more than any wedding could," he said in a deep, round voice, and again he dipped the comb into the water, "for the first time in a thousand years we in Croatia finally have our own independent state." With a sideways glance, Mijo checked out his own black cloth pants, white shirt, black blazer only a slightly different shade of black than the pants: *I must say, my clothes aren't half bad either*, he thought. He'd put on his best suit, the one he would be married in one day, when he and Drenka had their wedding. "What's the time?" asked the boy. Mijo glanced at the clock on the wall, but the man with the crutch said, "Well, it's only eight." The boy said, "Just so we're not late." "Hey, even if we were going to America we'd get there on time," said Mijo, warmed by the šljivovica and slowly pushing away the empty glass. The man nodded, again set his crutch aside, sat by the blazing metal stove, and put his skinny hands to work; pressing his knees together, he started shelling corn kernels. He coughed and said, "Son, do keep an eye out. I hear they've blown up the railway tracks near Blečići." The boy ran the comb decisively through his hair once more and said, frowning at the mirror, "If we're scared off by someone now that we have our own state, we have no right to be here." He leaned over, quickly pulled on his new tan army boots, jumped in them so they'd go all the way on, arranged his pantlegs over the boots, went out into the yard, and with both hands patted the dog's warm head. "Where'd you get those boots?" asked Mijo, feeling the thin soles of his own well-worn shoes. "Bring a lamb with you next time and I'll get you a pair," laughed the boy and tightened his belt. "Looks to me like those mathematics studies of yours in the city are going pretty well," Mijo thumped him on the back. Just then the man with the crutch poked his head out of the house and said, "Son, go show Mijo the horse we bought." "Come on, I'll show you," said the boy, but partway across the yard, a few meters from the new barn—the only one in the village that stood separate from the house—he was stopped by a woman's voice: "You'll start smelling like the barn if you go in there, wait to see the horse when you get back!" So the two of them stopped in their tracks, and the boy, looking over at the window where the voice came from, said, "Come on, hurry up, ready yet?" She quickly descended the slanting wooden staircase, wearing a white dress of stiff homespun linen with green branches and red roses embroidered on the collar and sleeves. "Just a minute while I put in more potatoes," she said and went back into the house. A few minutes later she brought out a knapsack she tossed to her brother, which he slung handily over his straight back. Then from somewhere in the house she pulled out an old cloth sack covered in patches, walked into the fenced-in chicken coop, strew a few kernels of corn on the ground, and when the chickens and two roosters began jostling the kernels with their claws—pecking at them and helping themselves—she circled around, grabbed the smaller rooster, all dirty from dust and mud, shoved it quickly into the sack, and tied it up with first one tug and then another. "Oh, Drenka dear, why him?" said the man with the crutch in the doorway, scraping his throat with a cough. "You've got yourself plenty of chickens to pick from, but that one crows for us so pretty every morning that he'd put a nightingale to shame with his song." She tightened her grip on the sack with the rooster in it and answered in a thin voice, "Well he's been attacking the chickens and the other day he went after me," she showed a drying scab on her hand from the rooster's sharp beak. Mijo swung the sack firmly over his shoulder, feeling on his back the wriggling of the furious rooster as it flapped its wings, and he thought, *having wings sure does help*. "Have you got water?" asked the man with the crutch and glanced up at the blue sky. "It'll be hot as hell out there today." "I do," Mijo pointed to the canteen hanging from the belt his father had passed down to him, along with the pants, the shirt, his eagle-beak of a nose—his dark eyes came from his mother, "and we'll fill them up at the Babina Greda spring when we pass by it." The sun had already reached its fullness when they started out toward the conifer forest, accompanied by the barking of the dog, which had perked up.

All three of them waved once more to the man with the crutch as they set off, and he raised his free hand and yelled after them, "Have yourselves a grand time!"

Rude walked first, fiddling with the pack on his back as if it chafed him, and Mijo and Drenka walked a few steps behind; mid-stride, Mijo fixed the sack that kept changing shape, then reached over and tenderly pinched the girl on the ribs; she stepped away and said, "Now it's time for you to walk ahead of me." Mijo laughed broadly at that. After they'd trudged over land harrowed into thick brown furrows and stepped into the trough of the road, Rude picked up the pace toward the forest. Mijo was again walking behind Drenka and told her, with his steps making a new sound, "It's wise for me to bring up the rear." It occurred to him she might take his words the wrong way so he added, more loudly, "So some wild animal doesn't come up on us from behind." He slowed a step or two behind so he could see her better; in her white dress, as if enveloped in snowy foam, among all those quivering leaves, bright flowers, gaudy butterflies, she looked like a forest queen;

when he saw the clouds scudding fast across the sky, Mijo thought it might be from the excitement he felt while he walked behind Drenka. As he ambled he suddenly shut his eyes and still more suddenly opened them, but now, to his surprise, there was not a single white cloud in the sky, just the sense of the smoothness of her rosy cheeks and shoulder blades sashaying with each other as she walked. Rude had increased the distance between them, from one tree to the next, he'd already moved on ahead, and now—while traversing a mown meadow, alive with brown moles that were moving, pulsing like the heart of the soil, like Mijo's heart—the two of them walked side by side, farther and farther behind Rude. Each time Mijo touched her hand tenderly, until she pulled away, he felt as if he were breathing through that hand of hers.

Drenka looked over at Mijo and, as she walked, said, "You've got a patch of fungus on your neck." He touched his neck. "Where?" and then, confused, he shrugged. At a slightly slower pace she said, "When we get back, I have some salve made from rabbit lard I can put on it." Then they picked up their pace to catch up with Rude and the distance shrank, but if they exchanged glances, it grew; by now they had come out onto a sunlit meadow full of blossoms. Mijo leaned over while walking and stealthily snapped off the crown of a flower in full bloom. First he thought to give it to her, but at the last minute he tucked it into his own hair. When the flower fell out both of them chuckled over it. They crossed a path sprinkled with yellow leaves, a small herd of cows across the meadow showed no movement or sound, but the voice of a shepherd sang out from the grove: "Oy, polenta, grown on rocky heights," mingled with the stirring wind. With a stab of hunger, Mijo finished the song: "Oh you taste so fine when cooked just right." It was only another fifty meters or so to the forest edge. Rude was sitting, short of breath, by a hazelnut shrub. Drenka was lagging behind, so Mijo stopped, waiting for her to come along, and then on the two of them went. "Can you manage?" he asked her, and she quickly replied, "Of course I can." When they caught up with Rude, Mijo sat down in the grass, breathing more slowly, and looked down at the village, surrounded by small patch-like lots, linked by invisible seams, and what with the looking he forgot to drink his water. He glanced over at the sack, pitted with five little holes that were like the rooster's multiple eyes. Just as Drenka sat, Rude got up and proceeded on. Mijo took the canteen, had a sip, and called after him, "What's the hurry, don't we still have time?" Rude stopped, broke a shaft of straw off from the side, stuck it in his mouth, and said, "I'm worrying we'll get lost." Mijo checked the sack with the rooster in it, which he had set down next to him. It was quiet, as if the rooster inside—having made peace with its fate—had dropped off to sleep. He poked a finger through one of the holes, widening it so the rooster would have more air. "Blindfolded I'd know my way through this forest." Rude said, "Better that way," and set off along the path marked by little caps of poisonous mushrooms, and when he vanished, the two of them got up and went into the forest after him; Mijo looked at his canteen, took another sip, and offered it to Drenka, but she shook her head. "Later." They caught up quickly with Rude, who was now walking more slowly because they couldn't see the path. Mijo's shirt was soaked through, he felt as if he had another layer of skin on his back, but the fresh breath of the forest felt very good. Rude was waiting for them by a tree that forked like a giant slingshot; it had wrangled room for itself in the forest. He pushed a stick into the rotten hollow; from it swarmed red ants; underfoot they had looked smaller. Again they set off slowly along the new narrow path that was quickly swallowed up by the abundant grass, but now Mijo was leading the way and Drenka was between them. They walked among huge beech trees with smooth gray bark, after each one there was another, even larger and thicker, so for a time they had to duck adroitly among them. "How long since you last came this way?" asked Rude, and Mijo said, "A clearing's just ahead." As he said that, sunlight shone through more brightly and they stepped out onto a nameless meadow, redolent of mountain grasses; Mijo breathed deeply and with the sharp smell he cleansed his wide-open nostrils. The sun beat down more harshly because there was no shade to be had in the middle of the bare saddle of the mountain except the shade the three of them cast for one another, so, as they walked through time slowed by the heat, they dodged the rays of the sun. Mijo took up his

canteen again, shook it, wetted his palm, moist-
ened the back of his head, and drank some water:
his mother had taught him that way when he was
a boy, after hard work in the fields, when he was
hot and very thirsty. Rude kept moving on, taking
up the lead, and at the forest—which began with
a stand of whiteish birch trees, followed by a pair
of tall pine trees growing up into sharp points
and then hundred-year-old oaks—he stopped
and said, "Where now?" As he passed Rude, Mijo
tossed him the sack with the rooster; Rude took
it begrudgingly and draped it over his shoulder
as Mijo said, "This way," and blazed ahead, first
with a sharp look, and then with his hand, feeling Drenka's eyes on his back, and he called to
them loudly over his shoulder, "Watch out for
branches so they don't scratch you in the face."
For the next half hour they forged their way in
silence through the dense virgin trees, overgrown
in moss and unaccustomed to people; from cracks
in the rocks, water sometimes sparked; as soon as
they broke free of the thicket they found themselves under the shady peak known as Pasji Vrh,
surrounded by a thick ring of fog and a meadow
full of white rocks, worn smooth by blasts of wind;

from afar these rocks with their uneven shapes looked like a scattered flock of sheep. According to tales told by the village elders, the rocks mark the graves of people who were slain in battles against the dreaded dog-heads of myth. On they swiftly moved from the mountain, also shaped like the head of a dog; Mijo thought how the mountain had been there since time immemorial. He hurried them along and, with the sack on his back, he waited for Drenka to pass and then stood protectively behind her, looking in fear at the mountains, for there were some in his village who still believed that far beneath—in the fissures among the stones, the sinkholes that reached down so deep they stretched all the way to hell itself—was where the dog-heads lived. The wind started gusting, blowing off the stone mountain, chasing sounds into the hollows, and for a moment it seemed to Mijo like the baying of the dog-heads. The forest they had now entered was full of taut branches. Once they'd moved far enough away from the rocks and traversed a stone gorge and a sloping meadow over which there buzzed invisible bees, they stopped by a lone wild apple tree to rest, gather their strength, drink some water. Mijo picked a squishy apple up from the grass in a cloud of fruit flies; he squeezed it in his fist until thick juice dripped from it and the juice smelled of apple brandy, the kind his father, while he was still alive, used to distill. As Rude and Drenka started off, Mijo grabbed an apple from a branch, ate it quickly, and trotted after them. A little later, by a spring swishing below cold, gray rocks, they filled both canteens, stopped, drank, listened to the burbling of the water; Mijo kneeled and after drinking from his cupped palms, he said, voice washed clean by the water, "It's blessed." Meanwhile, Drenka took the potatoes from Rude's pack and scrubbed them in the water, rinsing off the thickly caked mud. From behind, Mijo tickled her ear with a piece of straw, sniffing at her warm hair. "Come now, don't!" she said and shifted her weight. Mijo tossed the piece of straw behind him, took a muddy potato from her hand, and started scrubbing it in the water while grinning until finally her reflection in the water grinned back; Rude filled a canteen, took a gulp, looked at the sun, and said, "Let's go, folks, it's past noon."

They continued on their way, followed by a sudden wheeze of wind that soon died down, and the sun appeared again from behind clouds to scorch everything that was moving through the forest. The eyes of birds shone in the treetops, Mijo watched them while he walked; then by stomping he drove them off the branches, for they were black like ravens, and made him think of ominous birds and how one can never expect anything good from them in life. He was walking again behind Drenka, looking at the short-lived bugs and at her—how she walked as if she were dancing. Her dress caught on burrs; she took care to keep it from snagging on a branch. *This is a true miracle*, he thought, *that it hasn't yet torn*; soon they were trudging over dry pinecones, listening to the crunching sounds underfoot. They stopped by a bird's nest from which a fledgling had fallen, looking like a child's heart that had just begun to beat, and Mijo took it tenderly in his two hands and then shinnied nimbly up the tree to return it to the nest, feeling Drenka's warm gaze on his back. They stopped at one point briefly by a chipped boulder, next to many scattered hazelnut shells; evidently somebody else had recently been there. By a spreading beech tree Mijo stopped again, lowered the sack with the rooster in it, and declared loudly, "Know what? Let's have something tasty to eat." Drenka looked around, her eyes lingering on the sack, and said, a little breathless, "If you're hungry, we can do that." Rude took hold of a branch, bent it toward him, and said, "But how long will all this take?" Mijo gave a dry laugh. "It will take until we've eaten the rooster." He sat on a patch of green grass, lowered the sack next to him, untied it, and Drenka straightened up, saying, "Take care it doesn't run off!" "And where can it run off to?" asked Mijo. "There's nowhere for it to go." At that the rooster emerged slowly from the sack; it thrust out its breast, spread its flaming wings, bigger, more beautiful, grander than the rooster the girl had stuffed into the sack at home; it stretched its neck out even farther and crowed into the sky, varying the timbre. "Will you look at our rooster," said Rude, beginning to whistle and snapping his fingers around its head to the rhythm of the melody: the rooster bristled, then flapped its wings at his outstretched boot. Rude hopped back a step as Mijo laughed aloud, then Drenka went into the bushes, crouched on her heels, and reached to gather up dry kindling. When she came back, she dropped the branches from her arms, then collected dry grass. She crisscrossed several of the thinner twigs, arranged the grass under them, stood, and asked, "Rude, got that little pocketknife on you?" He dipped his hand deep into his pocket; pulling out a knife, he tossed it over to Mijo; Mijo had not expected it and he lunged as if catching a hot potato, but he caught the knife. He drew the blade out from the wooden sheath and said, faltering, "I can't be the one to butcher it." Rude grinned, looking right at him. "Anyone who can't butcher a rooster, can't defend his country." "So what about you?" said Mijo and very nearly tossed him back the pocketknife with the blade still open. Rude said, "I'd rather not get blood on my clothes." Mijo stood up and, cutting a twig from the hazelnut shrub, "So your clothes matter more than mine?" Drenka shot her brother a sideways glance, saying, "Come on, light the fire." She put her hand in her pocket and pulled out a few kernels of corn, said "pi, pi," and tossed them in front of her; the rooster made its way cautiously over to the corn. Peering around haughtily, it ate a kernel, moved on to peck at the next one. Drenka jumped forward, grabbing it with one hand by the neck, while with the other she firmly grasped its feet and tucked the bird under her arm. It thrashed, and with its shining feathers flying every which way she looked as if she were trying to rein in blazing flames under her arm. She went over to Mijo, took the pocketknife from his hand without a word, and carried the rooster to a fallen tree. She slapped it onto the trunk and pinned it under her bare, round knee. The rooster thrashed around again so Mijo came over quickly, grabbed the rooster with both hands and pressed it back to the bark. He said to her, "Give the knife here!" Drenka quickly passed him the knife, and next to his fingers that he had firmly wrapped around the rooster's neck, he swiftly cut it until its head, after one more pass with the knife, rolled off into the shining grass. With the rooster writhing in his hand Mijo crouched and wiped the knife clean in the grass. He looked over at Rude who was staring into the freshly budding fire; then he straightened up, gave Drenka the knife, and off she went into the underbrush. With sounds that were already sharp she sliced off a hazelnut branch from which she stripped the bark and whittled the tip to a point. Mijo was still holding the headless rooster: with each new spasm blood dripped from its neck. Mijo looked over at Rude again (still not exactly sure what he wanted to tell him with this look), who had crouched down by the fire and was blowing at it to get it going. He lowered the rooster down in front of him; it flopped first to the side, but then rose up on its tottering yellow legs, staggered around headless, then stretched its neck and only after several seconds toppled over into the grass, where it shuddered for a moment or two until it went utterly still. Drenka walked calmly over, took it between her hands, and began to dig her fingers deep into it, as if reshaping it, and when one more drop of blood had drained from the red tubes of its neck, she took it calmly by the feet, swung it twice, and tossed it closer to the now-blazing fire.

On they strode through the forest; nudging each other with thick breath from behind. "We're going the right way?" asked Rude as he pushed aside a slender branch with a long smooth leaf. "I'm having trouble because I ate too much of that rooster and now I can't walk as fast." Mijo looked at them with an expression that was meant to be a smile. He snapped off a twig and used it to clean his teeth, picking at the remaining tough fibers of meat. Drenka, meanwhile, crouched and with saliva on her finger she rubbed away at tiny droplets of blood on her sleeve. Mijo stopped, looked left, right, and set off again, saying in a dry voice, "Yes, this is right, straight on." He sucked loudly on one more morsel of meat, took the canteen, held a big swig of water in his mouth, swirled it around, and swallowed it slowly down to let Rude know there was no cause for alarm, though he did have the feeling that the trees hadn't been quite this tall when he'd passed through here last. But that was a full two months ago, when he had driven his cow to town to sell it. He walked, the two of them following; the forest grew denser, more silent, as if with a life of its own. Mijo kept stopping, hurrying his gaze around him; he listened and everything ahead and around him felt as if it could be familiar. Any minute now that particular tree was sure to make a rustling noise, a red-tailed bird soon would call brightly from another tree, like the bird he'd seen the last time, but none of these things did happen, except that the sun broke through the branches and sent him back his squint. The birds fell completely quiet, so all that could be heard were muffled steps and the pushing aside of sturdy plants crowned with sharp thorns; then they were walking through lichens and moss and every few steps they tripped on the heads of inquisitive white flowers that were peeking more often from the grass. Above them hung wild cherries, tiny, juicy, Mijo would gladly have paused, shinnied up, and crammed them all into his mouth, but he thought there would be time enough for cherries on the way back. From somewhere came a dragonfly; it arrived with one sound and left with another, vanishing into the dark space among the trees. Mijo stopped and waited for Drenka to rest a little, because she had stopped and again was scrubbing away at the bloodstain with her spit. When she started walking again, Mijo did too; as Rude walked he smoothed his suit jacket over his chest with his hands. Along a path hidden by grasses, that he also wasn't sure of, Mijo suddenly noticed crouching shadows like a dream that lasted as long as his gaze did: two men were darting through the underbrush. He stopped abruptly, and behind him

Drenka and Rude did too. Several more lurching shadows raced through the trees; then a woman with a child clutched to her bosom; her sighs mixing with gasping sobs. "What's this?" said Mijo, and Drenka replied, "Gypsies." "I know they're Gypsies," said Mijo. "But what are they running away from? They look so terrified." Rude stepped around a bedraggled bush and looked, then he said: "Gypsies? Who cares? But are you absolutely certain you know exactly where we are right now?" Mijo tore a leaf off a branch, blew his nose into it, then took his place as leader of the party, striding on ahead with confidence; he thought about the Gypsies; he'd considered calling, "Hello there," to them, asking how much farther it was to town. As he walked two squirrels were prancing and chasing one another around on a tree; first there, then gone, waving their flamboyant, brown tails.

Mijo parted the underbrush with his hands, Drenka and Rude walked behind him and did the same. "Almost there," said Mijo. "I believe we'll arrive in about an hour, possibly sooner." Then they left the forest that always seemed so dense that a wolf might get lost in it and they dove into a sea of undulating greenness, long grass, their heads barely visible: Drenka walked and every so often eyed the droplets of blood on the sleeve of her dress. "Pass me a little more water," she said to Mijo. He poured some onto the spot, and she rubbed it as she walked, but the bloodstain only spread all the more. "You'll wash it when we get there, every restroom there has soap," said Mijo. Rude pushed ahead; looking back at them over his shoulder, he said, "Come on, you two, let's pick up the pace." "Brother, we're going as fast as we can," said Drenka, sucking air through her nose to soften the anger in her voice. After her words Mijo felt an ever greater closeness to her; he could barely stop himself from giving her a big hug; they walked a little more through the waving grass. Then a valley full of hot air. Then again through the forest that was forever regenerating, Mijo was going faster, every intake of breath brought a new smell, with each smell a new view; in front of him he could already picture the small town, its genteel white houses, the boisterous taverns with the smell of beer foam. When they finally emerged from the forest, they could hear the occasional burst of music in the distance; they passed through fields of corn stalks as tall as people. All they had left to traverse to reach town was one steep hill, a brief fir-covered slope; along the road a lithesome stream emerged and zigzagged back and forth several times. Drenka went down to the water straightaway, took hold of the edge of her sleeve, and began scrubbing the bloodstain in the water. Mijo hurried her along, wiping grains of sweat from his brow, the droplets spraying around him, and again he said, "A little soap and that will come right out." Rude was already on a straight stretch of the road, deeply rutted by cartwheels: it branched off in all directions—in the shape of a family tree—onto smaller roads and pathways crowded with people, some of whom were carrying the tricolor flags of the new independent state on their long hoes.

Rude kept pulling ahead, and Drenka and Mijo were scarcely able to keep up. He snatched a clump of green grass and lengthened his step so he could reach down and polish his boots as he walked. At the next gentle curve Drenka and Mijo were passed along the roadside by a man on a bicycle with a rifle slung over his back, and—wanting to catch up with Rude—they passed an elderly man who was walking and every so often, with hands raised, carrying a shining picture of Jesus, he called out, "Oh, thank you, God! Oh, thank you, dear God!" Then, with the trample of unshod hooves and dust, a festive horse-drawn cart crammed with people passed, and then another; from beyond a plum orchard and closely ordered haystacks, a weaving oxcart joined the road, sending sparks from its cartwheels, and children greeted them, waving, from it—on their heads they were wearing paper army hats with the letter U for Ustaša drawn on each one. Mijo waved back to them, and together with Drenka, who was keeping her eyes trained on the path ahead, he sped up until, after a few minutes, they caught up with Rude. As they approached, they could see and hear quite clearly a crowd of people, then the strains of an accordion and dancers dressed in folk costumes, who—like the gears in the belly of a clock—were moving in circles and spinning, accelerating with rapid movements the steps of their dance as they closed in, faster and faster, on the festooned houses.

Father

BY THE TREE STOOD A TALL, THIN MAN, WEARING
a coat of dog hide; he was standing stock still,
had dug in his heels, as if he would forever be
apart from the world, and it seemed to him that
this flute-like sound from the mountain had to
do with something up in the mysterious heavens.
Then, through the rising howl of the wind, which
flapped his rag-like pantleg and sent rocks rolling
down the gullied road, he heard above him quite
a clear voice, which could have been God's voice:
DO IT! Bound by his stillness, he breathed in
deeply, then huffed sharply a few times into his
lined hands, rubbed them together, scooped water
in passing from the wooden bucket—and then
his life seemed split between what it had been
before he splashed his face with the clear, cold
water and what came after—nothing would be
the same after that and life would take off on an

entirely different tack—so once again, just in case, he splashed himself and smoothed his creased face. Then he slowly entered the house; the room was a square, the floor packed earth, in the middle there was a hearth surrounded by black stones, full of still-glowing embers that lit the uneven beams and the row of sharp wolves' teeth strung on a thread of spun wool, hung from a sooty rafter to guard against curses. In the corner of the room a small woman with translucent skin was dozing and rocking a baby in a cradle from where she was half-lying, half-sitting; right next to her there on the straw were three children slumbering under a colorful piece of cloth: a boy on one side, the little girls on the other. In the opposite corner, on a bed of straw covered with a sheepskin coat, lay a motionless old man, his beard full of red glints. The man crouched silently by the hearth, then from a wicker basket he took two heavy horn-beam logs and laid them one atop the other on the embers and blew vigorously to stir the fire. *At least there's firewood*, he thought, his eyes full of smoke; he rose, took a step back, and let a beam of daylight enter through a crack in the half-closed door. The fire quickly flickered and blazed, and the flaming tongues licked upward, changing and moving the shadows on the ceiling, so the room itself, from the fire and the dance of the shadows, seemed to sway and shift of its own accord. When the baby in the cradle suddenly began crying, the woman hastened to rock it faster, but to no avail. The children woke up at nearly the same moment, and—as if they were still dreaming—began tugging at the piece of cloth that covered them, kicking. The woman tried to soothe them with her hushed voice, but when they didn't stop, she reached for a switch, lashing at them with it; they ducked quickly under the covers (with only their bare feet sticking out). Again they began to fidget; when the man shouted, "Enough!" they went stiff as if turning to stone under the taut vault of the fabric. After shouting the man had difficulty breathing and through the thin slits of his eyes he watched the fire; then for a few more minutes he listened to the sound of the sporadic gusts of wind, which was, little by little, dying down. He put another log on the fire; with a bough he swept together the scattered embers, and then his gaze came to rest on a red copper cookpot, the only one in the house—the few potatoes they had left were cooking in it. During the winter snows, when you couldn't so much as poke your head out for the blizzards and ravenous wolves that lurked all around the house, they'd use the cookpot as a chamber pot, and during the day they'd cook in that same pot; *but soon*, he thought and a chill ran down his legs, *there would be no more shitting in this house*.

He rose, went out in front of the house, rubbed his face with his hand, and listened to the sound of a spoon scraping the bottom of a tin dish at his neighbor's house; to calm himself he clenched his fists and the bones in his hand made a noise as they moved; he closed his eyes. In the middle of his forehead appeared long, vertical creases as if carved by an invisible knife; again the wind pummeled fiercely; it bowed the sinewy branches of the trees to the ground, ripped old and new spiderwebs from the cracks in the wooden dwellings. The man mused on whether to go back in or stay a little longer outdoors; he began, with absentminded steps, to walk around the house; he dragged behind him his long and heavy legs. At the angular end of the house he suddenly stopped, not knowing what he'd do, where he'd go—for a moment it seemed like night, then day again coming from behind the house—and he studied his fingernails, caked with black and crusty mud; he leaned over, picked up a sliver of wood and went about prizing the greasy black soil from under his nails, the blood and mud mixing. He went over to a bucket of water and thoroughly washed his hands and bloody fingers. He looked at the sky, waiting for day to dawn over the village: he was eager to go off into the forest as soon as possible to check on the traps he'd reset the day before to catch hares. He had a feeling they'd be dining on hare that day and he had already begun to dream about sucking the morsels of meat from between his strong, white teeth, and his mouth watered, and because of all that spit he had to hawk it out.

Borne by thoughts of a hare turning on a spit, he began pacing faster around the house, then glanced—more with his brow than his eyes—toward the foggy mountain. He thought of his father as he strode along faster and more restive, and his head wagged loosely on his shoulders; it looked as if with each new step the detached jerks of his head merely confirmed his thoughts, that he ought do as the good Lord commanded. Other thoughts plagued him too: each beginning with the image of him carrying his father uphill on his back, bent over in a gentle curve, but he did not want to think any of these thoughts through to the end. He drew his coat tighter around him and began in his fractured posture on the threshing floor to collect the scattered tree bones, which the wind in its unbridled repetition had snapped.

A little later the man went into the house and straight away, from its hook by the door, he took his double-headed axe with the short handle, worn down by constant use. Sharply closing the door behind him, he slung the axe over his shoulder and set off without hesitation up the slope, on his way to the greening forest. High above flew black birds, traversing the backdrop of the sky as they flew in continually changing formations. He stopped, watched the long-necked birds with interest and tried to extract from the mysterious patterns some sort of meaning, but under his skin all that trembled was restlessness, so he ventured deeper into the forest. He was hindered as he walked by hanging vines, for—caught up by thoughts of food, birds, children—he took an altogether different and roundabout route to where he was going, a way nobody ever took; with precise blows of the axe he sliced his way through the sinewy obstacles and felt after each blow of the blade that he was not only walking faster, but breathing far more easily.

He fought his way out from the tangle of branches, the snarl of the long grasses, the loosened vines coiled around the old tree trunks, and then he moved on into a dense copse crisscrossed with nettles and lichen: he quickly, impatiently examined all three traps, hidden along barely visible paths, overgrown in the tall grass, along which he'd been certain that the hares, poking with those long, pointy ears of theirs, passed by daily. The traps were very simple, his father had always hunted that way; a noose of wire attached to the nearest tree. The week before a fox had been caught in one; he didn't see it, but he recognized its bloody paw. He tossed the paw into a nearby anthill. Who knows how long it jerked at its paw, breaking it off or gnawing it through until it freed itself, and momentarily he felt glad that it had, yes, for though the fox was also a pest, you couldn't eat it, so it was better that the poor thing pulled free. Then he remembered that it stole chickens—not that he had any chickens at home—and that left him feeling sorry that it hadn't choked to death. Several times over the last few years the same thing had happened on this very site, his quarry had been stolen from the noose: he knew from the bloody traces left on the wire, the tufts of stuck hair, and he suspected some of his fellow villagers. So he preferred to make the rounds of his traps early in the morning, before the sun had risen up from behind the hill and lit the village at its zenith. He arranged the empty nooses a little better on the ground, and spitting by his feet—an unvoiced curse accompanying every hawk—he sat down right in the leafy grass next to the nearest tree, a broken one. He sank his axe into another fir tree, upright, fresh, fragrant; he tore a piece of bark from it and chewed it, for he was momentarily overcome by unbearable hunger; chewing on the bitter-tasting bark, dreaming and imagining slivers of roasted bacon, he decided he'd go to his neighbor Toma's;

even though a month before, right here in this
very forest, perhaps on this same splintered tree
trunk, he could no longer recall, he'd vowed on
his children—indeed he'd sworn—that he would
sooner kill himself than ever again ask Toma for
anything. But if he persisted in his obstinacy, he
thought, everyone in his household would die of
hunger over the next few months; nobody would
survive the coming winter, and if it were a bad one
(the old women were saying it would be), then
nobody in the village, with the exception, perhaps,
of Toma—though even what he had in his larder
wasn't endless—would be safe. He spat again and
thought how in this world the only abundance
was of evil and trouble, and with these words he
was overcome by bleak and vague forebodings.

He gazed up at the roofs of the trees, which somewhere up there melted into the fog; he sniffed the
forest brimming with juice, everything seemed
so simple and within reach, yet still his hands
held nothing—he schemed over what he could
do, how to catch himself something. Then, to his
right he heard first a brief noise before his sharpened eye spotted it: a hare, long and gray, and his

face, at the sight, froze; he went quiet. The hare naively hopped straight toward the taut trap on the path. Hidden behind a bush, the man kept his eye trained on it, he approached it with his dark, motionless gaze, and in his eyes the hare was already caught; he squinted with one eye to draw the silence in all the more. The hare with its paws in the grass nudged the tense silence: it sniffed the trap on all sides, but did not put its paws in the noose, nor its head. It passed right by, even brushed the wire with its little tail as if mocking it, but then headed straight for the man. He silently raised the axe above his head and with his eyes full of unbridled force, he stood that way for a long time; full of vague twitches, the hare, in an instant, suddenly hopped like a released spring and bounded into the thick undergrowth. The man shot up from his crouch. In despair he shrieked and flung his axe after the hare, then swearing long and loud, he retrieved the axe from the bushes, once again checked his empty traps—though he knew they were empty—and set off back to the village. He could have wailed with despair; a few times while he was alone in the dense forest a gurgling sound came from his throat, his chest shook, but his eyes by some miracle stayed dry, as if with time he'd weaned himself from crying. He couldn't remember when he'd last squeezed from himself a single tear, perhaps when he was a boy and a cow had stepped on his foot, but even then he'd quickly had to stop crying because his father didn't allow it; his mother would thrust her head into a haystack behind the house when she felt tears coming on. Once when he was crying he rammed his head into corn husks; afterward he sneezed for days. The wind starting gusting again, the man began his descent. Along the way he sank his axe vengefully several times into healthy trees and brandished it left and right, up and down, assailing some invisible foe. He stopped suddenly and powerfully kicked a faded dog's skull, which, as it flew, spinning, looked at him through its dark sockets; he descended slowly and scanned the entire village with a broad sweep; the ground creaked loudly and absorbed his ever more rapid steps. As he walked he surveyed his patch of grayish and lumpy soil, scorched to the point of nullity, which he'd wrested, years before, from the brambles. When he came to the threshing floor, after walking over newly sprouted mole hills, he immediately leaned his axe on the wooden wall of the house and without hesitating he walked with tight steps to Toma's, bent, nevertheless, on asking.

He soon arrived at a house much like his own; in the fenced-in yard, on a stump planted firmly on the ground, sat a balding man who was fiddling with an ox cart missing its right wheel. "Toma, I'll be needing a little more," he said, slowly halting and nudging the dry goat turds in front of him with his feet. "I have nothing left," replied the long, black whiskers, "and you still have to return what you took before." "My children are hungry," he said in a low voice. "So'll be mine if I'm not careful," said Toma and spun the wheel, as if by doing this he was settling up their final accounts; then he rose to his feet, brushed off his pantlegs, and walked slowly, without a word, into the house. He poked his head back out for a moment, pointed to the tobacco pouch in his hand, and said, "All I can give you is a little tobacco, if you like?" And the man muttered through clenched teeth, "I'll take nothing of yours." He kicked the stump, pushing off from it, and walked rapidly away, angry at himself that he'd gone to Toma to ask for anything.

The man went back to his house; a little later he heard wails coming from the end of the village. He looked out and saw a woman, her hair in disarray, her lips bloody from biting them, and with her a bareheaded man. Between them they were carrying a white bundle across the mown clearing where children were buried: yet another child had died in the village, the third in the past week. He crossed himself and with fear he watched the two dark figures as they scrabbled in a frenzy with their hands in the dirt then lowered the child into the shallow grave; he turned away from the scene and their loud keening and saw his own children, who were just coming out of the house, jostling each other, raising thick yellow dust around them. His wife also came out with the baby in her arms, her hair loose, unruly, which he saw as a bad omen. "Put your hair up!" he snapped at her, raising his voice. She said, "Hair doesn't matter." He shouted, "Put up your hair or I'll chop it off with my axe!" His wife went quickly back into the house and came out with her hair done up firmly in a ponytail. The baby pressed close against her, nuzzled, trying to latch onto her breast, but she kept pulling away because she had no milk left:

she took an onion from her pocket and gave it to the baby to suck on to ease its hunger pangs at least a little. The man waited for the children to stop pushing each other; he stood near his wife, turning his back to her and staring up at the rocky mountain over which wisps of fogs were touching. When the children went back into the house, he said, "Ah." His wife said, "Mm." "Say anything?" he asked. "Nope," she said, her voice trembling, and she closed her eyes and began to cry without a sound. The baby kept pestering for her breast, so again she offered the onion bulb, already wrinkled and yellow, brushing away thin streaks of tears with her hand. "Don't you be crying now," said the man; he came over to his wife and baby. He caressed the baby with his eyes and began to walk his fingers along the bare arm, feeling in each finger the muffled heartbeat. The baby watched the man's marching fingers with interest, then began to cry, eyes squeezed shut and thin little legs moving, which looked more like the legs of a large insect than of a child. His wife, her eyes glassy from tears, more fiercely pressed the onion bulb into the baby's mouth, whom she held even more tightly in her arms, but again the man looked away; he turned all the way around and, unnaturally upright, he watched the children, who had come out and begun romping again. Suddenly he barked, "Enough!" and the word flew around the house a few times; the children stopped in their tracks and watched him, out of breath. "You're just stirring up a mess with all the dust!" he shouted because he didn't want to say, *Don't waste your strength for nothing.* The children were still panting while sneaking glances at each other and giggling; into the house he went, with the baby's wailing reverberating louder between the walls of his skull; he latched the door to block out the crying, sat by the burned-down fire, and forced himself to poke at it with a piece of twig because he no longer knew where to go with his hands and eyes. In the ashy light the old man slowly opened his eyes deeply set in their sockets; he rose up and leaned his head against a log, all black from the damp, as if about to make a grand announcement. "Son," he said, "no point in waiting. Torment for all of you and for me." The man chose not to hear the words; he snapped off the twig, tossed it into the fire, watched it burn, and every now and then a shadow on the wall nibbled at the light, and each time the nibble stabbed him sharply in the chest. In silence he took the earthenware pitcher, and had a drink of water from it, wiping his wet mouth with his sleeve. The old man, like a moving shadow, sank down again with effort under the sheepskin coat; the man jumped up suddenly, grasped the old man firmly under the arms, and pivoted him on his wobbly legs; the old man's sharp, protruding shoulder blades on his back looked as if they were about to pierce clean through his pale skin. The man then patiently helped the old man sit on the round, three-legged stool; he went to the cupboard—which he himself had carved three years before from hard beechwood—stood on his tiptoes, took from the highest shelf a small lump of cheese wrapped in a green pumpkin leaf, and offered it to the old man. "Don't," said the old man with a half-breath, "what good will it do for this dead man? Give it to the little ones."

As soon as day broke, he went out in front of the house and sat on a rock; breathing through his open mouth, he watched the sun come up from behind the hill. He took off his fur hat with ear flaps, trying to smile to the sun, but the right side of his face tightened. He began to think he might ask Toma again for a little food. The thought made him itch, so he rolled up his sleeve and with his teeth he bit his flesh in order to scratch all the better on that spot. He got up, rolled the sleeve back down with his hand, then inside himself he uttered the sentence, "Give me a little more," but when he mouthed the word "Toma," he spat it out abruptly, shouting for the whole village to hear. "May they all die..." And the wind finished his sentence.

***

The man recoiled, brusque and full of rage—while rays of sunlight insinuated themselves through cracks in the roughly hewn boards of the door, and the colors of darkness moved slowly from object to object—as he helped the old man put on a tunic of tightly woven village homespun fabric and firmly fastened a goathair rope around his waist. With a single hoist he lifted the old man up onto his back. The old man clutched him around the neck and pressed the length of his body to his curving back. The man bent the upper part of his body over even further and with shuffling steps he slipped by his sleeping children and his wife who averted her eyes; he opened the door and with his heel he slowly drew it closed with a muffled squeak. He carried the old man on his back toward the mountain, which in the early morning light looked like a rooster's red comb. While he carried him, bone confronted bone but nothing abraded the man, he didn't think about a thing, all he cared about was reaching the round stone pit surrounded by thick ferns as soon as possible: to do it and then come quickly home. At times on his way up the gentle slope above his house he looked over at the nearby sun, which was growing larger; sweat poured down his brow and cheeks, pooling in the hollow of his neck, stinging his skin. The old man was scrawny, contorted, but somehow heavy, and after they'd gone halfway, the man began stopping more often. He'd gather his shaky steps, and then be overcome by rage and from his rage he'd draw new strength, bringing his steps to a decisive and steady pace. The village in the motionless heat lay farther and farther behind, and the transparent fogs kept reviving; in some places these fogs turned into white-hued rings like heavenly wheels, and, doggedly following their plod, drew the men with each new step away from the village. At one steep incline the man, his lips twisted at an angle, bit leaves off of a hazelnut bush as he walked by, chewed, swallowed, then stopped to rest a little. Then, at the edge of his field of vision, the boy suddenly turned up. "Mijo!" yelled the man, spitting out the leaves and stomping his foot on the ground, sharpening his words. "Where are you off to?" The boy ran to him, panting. "I'm going with you!" he blurted. The man first tried to drive him straight back home with a glare. Then, at a loss for words, he jerked his foot and just barked in a hard voice, "Home!" The boy stepped back reluctantly, stood by a branching beech tree that hung down all around him, and his slightly larger trembling lower lip sagged as if at any minute he'd start to cry. The man bore down on the boy with a new, furious glare, then he howled, biting his tongue and with the last word drawn out and all green from the leaves he'd been chewing: "What did I saaaaay?" All the while the old man was mumbling something, it might have been a prayer, but the man didn't understand a word of it. The boy, with uneven movements—each a plea for forgiveness, or so the man told himself—turned and quickly vanished into the thick hazelnut shrubbery.

When, along with the chorus of sizzling crickets, the man carrying the old man trudged on up a steep new path full of wilted flowers, the boy shadowed them along the dark edge of the fir forest, and the man, whose eyes were constantly moving, kept track of him. Between two long strides his fractured memory came back, and he was not comfortable remembering how he, as a boy, had followed his own father who'd carried his grandfather uphill; he looked around, but his gaze, despite his will, kept sticking to that memory that he'd stowed away. His father had told him to wait by a dogwood bush while he took care of something. He'd be leaving the grandfather, who would stay to live by himself for a time in the forest; yet the man, when he was a boy, knew full well that his father would throw his grandfather into the maw of the bottomless pit, that this simply had to be. The man, between two blinks or even quicker, noticed to one side a mighty tree in its full height,

and remembered how his father with his grandfather on his back had spotted a wolf lurking in
the bushes, baring its teeth, and how he'd chased
it off with loud shouts and by stomping his foot.
He looked at the boy, who was slinking along
as if constantly seeking, with each step, a more
secure foothold. "Hey, come over here!" he called,
and the boy laughed with joy, swallowed his grin,
hopped, and ran with short, rapid steps. The man
shifted the old man to a better hold on his back,
feeling the old man's heavy breath on his neck;
on they walked and through the whiteness of the
day they gradually conquered territory, moving
through the torrent of dense, green forest, full of
black spruce trees, ash-gray birches, and young
hornbeams. They inhaled the breath of the forest;
at one moment the trees looked as though their
roots were growing upward, or so it seemed to the
man in the baking heat. Then after a half hour,
their bodies overheated, they passed a downed
and trimmed tree and arrived at gravelly soil, then
through a rocky gorge they followed footholds
that continued along a narrow ledge of taut path
and then among hot cliffs whose walls were lined
with dried moss on both sides, blackened by the

sun. Again they came out in a cooler, wooded stretch, where the trees were overgrown by climbing vines with tiny blue leaves; a breeze picked up just then, stretching the sun's shadows, heightening the smell of the coniferous woodland. From all sides they smelled the fragrance of the resin that oozed down the green torches of the firs, which gave them strength, and under their feet rustled straw-like dry grass. The boy kept prancing around the man and the old man—the distance between them grew, then shrank. He hopped as if weightless and with him hopped the sun and the green, thumb-sized grasshoppers that awkwardly collided mid-air. The sun beat down mercilessly; the weblike shadows of the trees etched themselves deep into the scorched earth and baked rocks, beaten by lightning and sprayed with sun stains, and the man again bit a leaf off of a tree he didn't recognize, but when he'd chewed it, the leaf was so bitter that he had to spit it out, long and hard, gagging loudly.

They stepped out into a barren area, not a single blade of grass except charred stumps and gaping crevices; sticky heat in the form of thick steam poured out of the many clefts in the ground, red and lumpy like congealed blood, so as he walked the man thought, *this is what hell looks like*. On they walked and mounted the steep, twisting path, with only the occasional sprouts of grass. They rested a little and then sped up, listening to the quickened tapping of the beak of a bird on a tree—as if the gears of a clock mechanism were ticking in a hollow, warning them to pick up the pace so nightfall wouldn't catch them on their way back. The breeze wafted through, each time from a different direction, and one sound was quickly joined by another, so that everything around them gave off deafening noise; the lead-gray color of the man's eyes quickly equaled the color of the sky; the sun had ducked momentarily behind clouds and rain began to fall; with the powerful, whipping swirl of the wind it fell horizontally, vertically, but always like sharp needles, and the man, led by flashing lightning—his gaze repeat-edly coming back to the wet boy—walked along the straight, disjointed path and with his eyes he sought some sort of protected place, but he had no thoughts of stopping. He walked, looking first at the boy, who was shielding himself from the rain with raised elbows, and then at his own drenched leather footwear; the rain fell and through the curtain of needlelike sounds they slogged deeper and deeper in the mud. Once it had soaked them to the skin and softened and obstructed the path, turning it into an earthen gruel that stuck to the feet, it finally stopped falling. But at least with their mouths facing skyward they'd slaked their thirst; only the old man stayed the entire time in that same motionless position, with his head leaning on the man's shoulder. Again the same sun reappeared, baking with its fat, lengthwise stripes even more fiercely than it had before the rainfall, quickly drying out the clothes that had glued firmly to their skins; suddenly a colorful butterfly appeared from somewhere; the boy went jumping after it, reached for it with his hands, wanted to catch it quickly. It brought joy into each of his movements, but the butterfly was always an instant faster, as if teasing him the whole time with its dizzying flits of direction; then it hid among the colorful forest flowers. After that it flew out, its wings even more translucent, and— followed by the child's laughter, which rang out for a long time—it vanished in the sun's light.

His back and knees bent, the man plodded uphill, holding the old man on his back and occasionally with unmatched eyes—one of them bloody from a burst capillary, the other dark and squinting from the scorch of the sun—he glanced at the boy. He found strength in looking back so he immediately sped up and, loudly huffing, under his feet he tamed the sinewy spear-like grass, which kept bouncing back up and righting itself, ever stronger and sharper. From the effort in his chest the man puffed his flushed cheeks and sharply blew out hot air; his ears were deafened by his own breathing; he stumbled and thought of his children, his wife, his house, the village, the oxen he would one day have in his barn, the cows' udders full of rich milk. The images kept swirling through his mind; again he turned his head to check where the boy was. He stopped, planting himself on his more robust right leg; the old man was still on his back, and with his breathing coming in gasps he looked back at the boy who, having melted into his own bent-over shadow with an invisible burden on his back, walked behind him, imitating in every detail what the man was doing—now the boy stood there calmly in the same bent-over pose, panting and looking around. The man was looking unblinkingly at him, he bent over a little more, glancing up at the sky as if into a cloudy mirror, and with the old man on his back he continued trudging on, as the boy in the same bent position slowly trudged on behind him.

DAMIR KARAKAŠ worked as a journalist and a war reporter from warfronts in Croatia, Bosnia, and Kosovo. In 2000 he published his first novel, *Kombetars* (2000), and later a short-story collection, *Kino Lika* (2001), which earned cult status on the Croatian literary scene. His writing has been translated into numerous languages, and his work has appeared in some of the most prominent international literary magazines. He lives in Zagreb.

ELLEN ELIAS-BURSAĆ translates fiction and nonfiction from the Bosnian, Croatian, Montenegrin, and Serbian. In 2006 the novel *Götz and Meyer* by David Albahari in her translation from the Serbian was given the National Translation Award. She is a past president of the American Literary Translators Association.